NANOOK

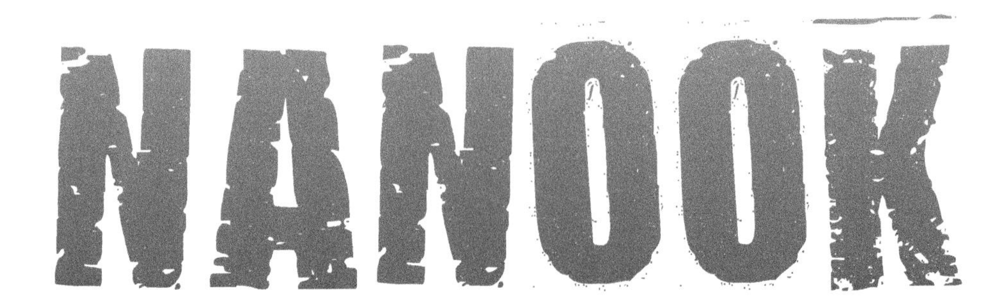

WRITTEN BY
LARRY HULSEY AND AUSTIN HULSEY

ILLUSTRATED BY
KYLE McCLOUD

NEW YORK
LONDON • NASHVILLE • MELBOURNE • VANCOUVER

Nanook

Published in New York, New York, by Morgan James Publishing. Morgan James is a trademark of Morgan James, LLC. www.MorganJamesPublishing.com

The Morgan James Speakers Group can bring authors to your live event. For more information or to book an event visit The Morgan James Speakers Group at www.TheMorganJamesSpeakersGroup.com.

ISBN 9781683506775 paperback
ISBN 9781683506782 eBook
Library of Congress Control Number: 2017911510

Cover and Interior Design by:
Chris Treccani
www.3dogcreative.net

In an effort to support local communities, raise awareness and funds, Morgan James Publishing donates a percentage of all book sales for the life of each book to Habitat for Humanity Peninsula and Greater Williamsburg.

Get involved today! Visit www.MorganJamesBuilds.com.

DEDICATION

This book is dedicated to my amazing children Parker-Raye and Rylan.
I am so proud of you both. Never give up on your dreams!
Remember to love, believe, trust, and live, truly live!

I love you!

Daddy

A NOTE FROM AUSTIN

A relationship with their father is one of the most influential relationships in a child's life. It's been over 25 years since the first time my dad told me the bedtime story of Nanook, and it has stayed with me ever since. As I grew and become a father myself, I passed the story of Nanook down to my children and could see the excitement and love in their eyes every time I spoke the story into their minds. It was my daughter who one night said, "Dad, why don't you and Papaw make this into a book so we can have it forever and share it with our friends?"

That was the spark that set this book towards becoming a reality, and I couldn't be more grateful for being able to see the story that touched my life as a child have the potential to touch the hearts of others across the world.

Thanks Dad for being so awesome. This book would have never happened without your willingness to give a child an imaginative adventure at bedtime.

Anyone can be a father, but it takes someone special to be a dad! Thanks Dad. I love you.

Austin

Father's Day 2017

A NOTE FROM LARRY

Thank God for a son that had enough foresight and love for the story of Nanook to give me a call and ask, "can we write Nanook?" And so, we did. I hope children everywhere will love the story and message Nanook will bring to them, and will remember it for years to come. I am so glad my son had the vision 25 years later to bring Nanook to life. I pray Nanook puts that same look of excitement and love for the story on every child's face!

Larry

Father's Day 2017

Babook knelt in the fresh snow that had fallen in April. He was carefully cleaning the gun his family had given him. It was an 1891 Russian Mosin-Nagant rifle. His family got it from the Russians when there was a large fur trade.

Babook was very proud of the gun because it helped feed his family for fifty years. He would pass it down to Nanook when he was older. This way the gun would stay in the family.

Nanook was born in the winter of 1934, when hunting and fishing were required for survival. There was no other way for his family to get food.

Nanook was twelve years old now, and he was a happy and helpful son. He had big rosy red cheeks that brightened his smile and held his father's love. Nanook loved to help his father gather firewood and do jobs around the village.

The coming days would test Nanook. They would make sure that he was ready to provide for his family and village. Nanook was a good fisherman, but he didn't like to wait. He loved to fish when they were biting, but he was bored when they weren't.

A cold wind mixed with snowflakes howled across the Alaskan tundra. Nanook stared out of the igloo window at the rising sun that promised a beautiful day for fishing.

Nanook and his father had been coming to the hunting and fishing camp in April for three years. Their village was less than two miles away, so they could easily reach it to get more bait and supplies.

Nanook had been dreaming of this trip for days because he knew he would get to leave the igloo. He also knew the salmon would be swimming in the river near camp.

The smaller salmon did not make the trip to the sea until they were larger. These smaller ones were what he liked to catch because they tasted better and were the perfect size for eating. Babook took him to Bear Mountain to fish before and Nanook caught many nice salmon there. Looking out his window, Nanook saw his father preparing for his trip to the village. Nanook was happy. He knew he was going fishing.

Nanook ran to his father's side to ask if he could go fishing. He was pleased because his father promised to let him go alone if he did all of his chores. He had to fish at Big Bend on the Canning River because it was safer.

"Father! Father! May I go fishing today like you promised?"

"Yes, son, as long as you go to Big Bend where the polar bears do not go."

Babook knew the polar bears liked to fish in the rapids near Bear Mountain. He banned Nanook from going there because that was where Old One Ear fished. He was the biggest, meanest polar bear in the tundra.

Babook shot Old One Ear's ear off at Bear Mountain when the bear was trying to steal the fish he caught a few years before. Babook hoped he would never see him again ..... **EVER!**

After promising his dad that he would only go to Big Bend to fish, Nanook began walking. His dad returned to the village to get supplies. Nanook walked fast across the fresh fallen snow. He left tracks as he went.

Nannook was at Big Bend in thirty minutes and started to fish in the slow moving water.

He fished for an hour without a single bite.
He grew bored.

The sun felt so warm shining on Nanook's back that it made him sleepy.

His thoughts wandered to Bear Mountain. Nanook forgot Babook's warning. Thoughts of catching fish filled his head.

Nanook knew he shouldn't go, but he thought he could be home before his father returned.

He could just walk up river and be there in less than an hour, so he set out walking as fast as he could. All he thought about was fish.

He arrived at the rapids and began fishing for the salmon that he could see swimming in the fast-moving water. He forgot about his father's warning.

The sun warmed his back as he caught three, four, and then five salmon.

Nanook noticed his shadow in the snow in front of him close to the water's edge. He watched as the fish suddenly stopped biting. He decided to gather his fish and start for home.

Nanook made one more cast and the bait hit the water with a splash. Only the river made a noise as the sun warmed his back.

Nanook was getting sleepy. He heard a loud **CRUNCH** that only a footstep in the snow would make. His heart started to beat faster and a chill ran down his neck. He could only think bear.

Oh no, please, not a bear. Another loud **CRUNCH** filled his ears. Nanook froze. He was frightened. He heard another **CRUNCH**. Then he heard the sound of something very big behind him.

Nanook stood there terrified. Then he heard **CRUNCH**, **CRUNCH**, **CRUNCH**, from farther away. Oh no, not another bear, he thought.

After another loud **CRUNCH**, Nanook could hear the bear's breathing and smell fish on its breath. Then he saw another shadow growing in the snow. It was a bear's head with a missing ear.

Old One Ear would **EAT** him for sure. Nanook was about to pass out from fright when a gun went **BANG!**

The bear howled, then growled, and then ran away as fast as he could! Babook shot at Old One Ear just before he grabbed Nanook. Babook shouted, "Nanook, come here my son!" Nanook turned and saw his father. He ran to him crying.

Babook sat Nanook down and told him he loved him very, very much.

He told him that he said to only fish at Big Bend because he was afraid Old One Ear would show up at Bear Mountain again.

"Promise me, son, that you will do as I ask from now on," Babook said. "I only give you rules to protect you because I love you very much. Thank God for the fresh fallen snow. Because of it, I was able to follow your tracks."

"I promise, Daddy," said Nanook. "I love you too." --

As they were leaving, Babook found half a polar bear's ear in the snow. He picked it up and handed it to Nanook. "Dry this, my son, and hang it in your bedroom so you remember this day forever, " Babook said.

Babook and Nanook never saw Old No Ears again.

ABOUT LARRY

Larry Hulsey was born on August 6,1956, and has lived in Nashville, Tennessee most of his life. Larry has worked in the automotive industry, most recently in local motorcycle industry, in Southern Kentucky and Middle Tennessee areas. He is the father of co-author Austin Hulsey, and has two beautiful grandchildren: Rylan and Parker-Raye Hulsey. Larry hopes he and Austin's story will touch the heart of many young children and inspire their dads to read it to them as a bedtime story.

ABOUT AUSTIN

Austin Hulsey is a serial entrepreneur in the fitness and nutrition industry. He is the CEO and Founder of Nutrifitt, a natural sports supplement and nutrition company in Nashville, Tennessee, as well as a founding partner in Apollo Nutrition, which specializes in therapeutic foods for medical establishments and individuals.

Austin holds a Bachelor of Science in Dietetics from Tennessee State University, where he was the author of the university's food and nutrition newsletter during college. He has been featured on numerous radio shows and podcasts to speak about entrepreneurship and nutrition. Austin enjoys staying active, weightlifting, rock climbing, hiking, and the adventures of life! He is a devoted father to his two children: Parker-Raye and Rylan.

ABOUT THE ILLUSTRATOR

Kyle McCloud is a professional illustrator and designer in Nashville, Tennessee, and is co-author Austin Hulsey's cousin. Kyle began drawing at 3 or 4 years old, and it was a fun experience for him right from the start. He continued drawing throughout his childhood, usually practicing by drawing his favorite characters from the TV shows he enjoyed. Art became an outlet and hobby as he continued exploring his skills. Kyle's parents always supported and praised his work, which drove him to pursue it even further. After high school, he earned a Bachelor of Arts in Illustration from the Nossi College of Art in Nashville. With years of practice and hard work under his belt, Kyle can now do what he loves for a living and for all his readers!

FOR THE DEVELOPING WORLD
LIBRARY
FOR ALL
DIGITAL LIBRARY

Printed in the USA
CPSIA information can be obtained
at www.ICGtesting.com
JSHW072031080923
47940JS00042B/580

9 781683 506775